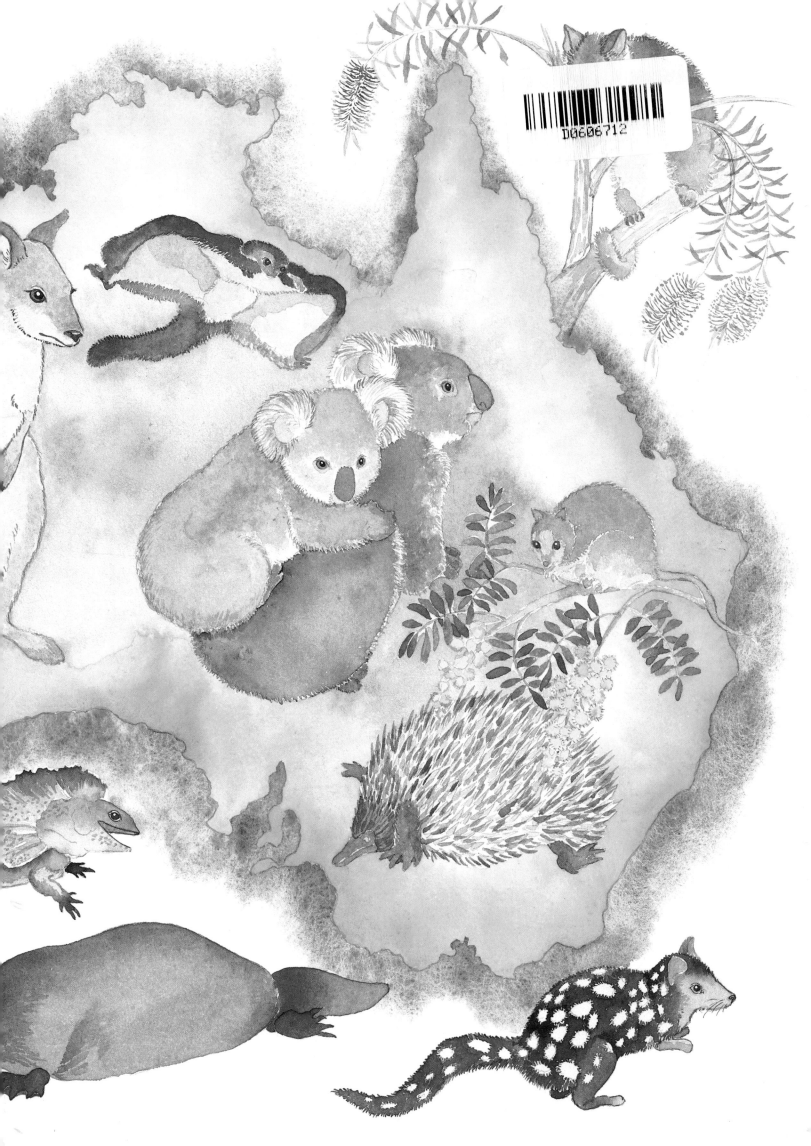

KYLIE'S SONG

Written by **Patty Sheehan**

Illustrated by **Itoko Maeno**

Advocacy Press • Santa Barbara

Dedicated to my Mother and
Father who understand what this
book is all about.

Published by Advocacy Press
P.O. Box 236
Santa Barbara, California 93102 USA

Library of Congress Cataloging-in-Publication Data
88-16779

ISBN 0-911655-19-0

Printed in Hong Kong

girls inc. *Advocacy Press is a division of Girls Incorporated of Greater Santa Barbara,*
an affiliate of Girls Incorporated of America.

Mama Koala was worried. You see, her baby didn't act like the other baby koalas. While they seldom made any sounds except perhaps to cry a little, her daughter Kylie . . .

sang. She sang every night, all night long. And the older Kylie grew, the louder she sang. She even made up songs to share about the other animals she saw from her tree in the Australian eucalyptus forest.

> *The Emu chicks don't have a nest,*
> *But papa guards them as they rest.*
> *Wallaby hops across the ground,*
> *Eating roots that he has found.*
>
> *Paddling with her big webbed feet,*
> *Platypus finds fish and bugs to eat.*
> *The Kookaburra laughs at everything.*
> *He's a bird who does not sing.*

Mama Koala loved the pretty songs. But . . .

"Surely," she thought, "other forest creatures will make fun of Kylie for singing and hurt her feelings." Mama was right.

Clarence, the grouchy old koala in the next tree would grunt to the other koalas, "I've never seen or heard of a singing koala. Koalas are not supposed to sing."

Then the other koalas would turn away from Kylie grumbling, "That's right. Koalas aren't supposed to sing."

But Kylie didn't notice. She kept right on singing. With her eyes sparkling and her head thrown back, she sang and sang. Singing was what she loved to do. She dreamed of growing up to be a great singer in her very own tree.

Mama Koala kept right on worrying. "How can Kylie be happy," she thought, "if no one likes her?"

Then, what Mama feared most happened.

The rude kookaburra, that bird who couldn't sing, was so jealous when he heard Kylie's pretty voice that he squawked

What a surprise. What a surprise.
I can't believe my ears and eyes.
Kylie sings just like a bird.
Funniest thing I ever heard.

All the other koalas began to laugh at her, and Kylie was hurt by their teasing. For the first time she had discovered that she was different. "No one likes me," she thought. She felt alone and sad.

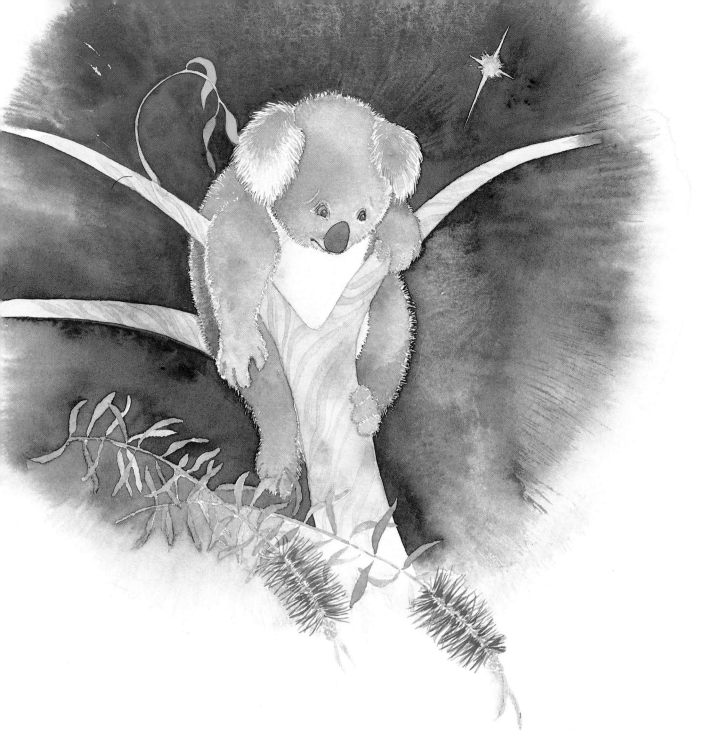

Poor Kylie. Sadly she crept way out on a long, lonely branch and sobbed to herself. "How can I stop singing? It's what I want to do. Why don't the others like my singing? There must be someone out there who wants to hear my songs."

Just then she heard a voice singing happily from far across the stream. "It's singing to me," Kylie thought. She was so excited she didn't notice that the branch she sat on had begun to sway dangerously in the rising wind.

Kylie sang back:

> *Who are you across the stream*
> *Singing that lovely song*
> *Please come close and be my friend*
> *So I can sing along.*

But the singing across the stream suddenly
stopped, and all Kylie heard was the screeching
of the rude kookaburra:

Kylie you are quite a sight
Singing and swinging in the night!
But in case you haven't heard,
You're a Koala, not a bird!

Before Kylie could answer . . .

The wind grew fierce and the rain beat down. As a bolt of lightning cracked the sky, Kylie's branch snapped and fell. Kylie grabbed for another branch and dangled there high above the forest floor. The other forest creatures, safe in their shelters, peeked out timidly to see what had happened.

Kylie clung to the branch, too frightened to make a sound. Mama Koala clutched her heart and begged Kylie to hang on tightly.

Finally the rain stopped and an exhausted Kylie climbed safely to Mama Koala's waiting arms.

"This wouldn't have happened if you hadn't been singing," Clarence called out.

"You know, Kylie," Mama Koala said as she comforted her frightened daughter, "Once I wanted to sing too. But, it's hard to be different. So I decided to be like the other koalas. Maybe that's what you should do."

Kylie didn't sing anymore that night. She didn't make a sound. The only voice she heard was inside her head: "I'll never sing again," it said over and over as she drifted off to sleep. "I'll never sing again."

As the months passed, the silent Kylie fit right in with the other koalas. But Mama Koala could see that Kylie was not the happy koala she had once been. Often, Mama Koala would find Kylie sitting alone staring sadly across the stream, searching with her eyes and ears for the spot where she had heard the beautiful answer to her song.

Mama Koala knew that Kylie would soon leave the tree to find a home of her own. She wanted to send her daughter off with the kind of advice that would help her to be happy. But what could she tell her? To be like the other koalas? Or to do what she loved, even if others didn't approve?

Mama Koala thought and thought. Finally on Kylie's last night at home, she made a decision. "I think you should find a tree where you can sing," she told Kylie. "You need to do the thing you love."

But Kylie remembered how sad and lonely she was when everybody laughed at her. "Maybe I'm not supposed to sing," she said, "but I can listen. I'll find the one who sang to me from across the stream."

As Kylie shinnied down the tree to begin her new life, Mama Koala called out encouragingly, "I just want you to be happy."

"Don't worry," Kylie called back to her. "I'll be fine. I love you Mama."

Kylie hadn't gone far when she came upon a most amazing sight! There before her eyes was a platypus drumming wonderful rhythms on a log with her big webbed feet. A wallaby was dancing to the music.

"Excuse me, mate," the wallaby called out, "Would you like to dance?"

Taken aback by the strange sight, Kylie shied away in surprise. "I've never seen a wallaby dance before!" she stammered. "And I thought platypuses only swam in streams and lived in burrows!"

"Well, I'm one wallaby who dances. Look at these legs. It seems that dancing is what they're made to do. And I love to dance."

"And I always dreamed of being a great drummer," said the platypus. "Now that my babies are grown up, I have plenty of time to practice."

"Well, I love to sing," said Kylie. "I want to be a great singer, and I have lots of time to practice. If a wallaby can dance and a platypus can drum, then a koala can sing if she wants to." Kylie was so happy that she sang out.

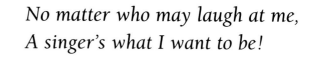

No matter who may laugh at me,
A singer's what I want to be!

"Bravo, bravo," Kylie's new friends called out.

"You have a lovely voice," said the platypus. "With training you could be a wonderful singer. You should meet Willie. He can teach you."

"Listen," said the wallaby. "You can hear him now across the stream."

Kylie listened. She did hear a voice . . . the same voice she'd heard singing to her so long ago!

Thanking her friends, Kylie plunged into the stream, swam across, and climbed a tall eucalyptus tree on the other side. She sang out:

> *I have come across the stream*
> *To learn your lovely song.*
> *Willie, won't you please teach me,*
> *So I can sing along.*

There was a rustling in the leaves as a bright-eyed, perky bird flew toward Kylie and perched himself on her branch. "I'm Willie Wagtail," he said. "I heard your pretty singing, and I will teach you all I know. But to be truly happy you must sing your own song, and you must learn to sing it well. Then others who love singing will find you."

Night after night, Kylie practiced her song with Willie's guidance. It was hard work. She practiced high notes and low notes, scales and deep breathing. She learned about rhythm and harmony.

It was worth all the work because Kylie became the best singer she could be. When she completed her lessons with Willie, she once again began to sing for the other animals. Kylie's song brought happiness to them each evening as it echoed through the forest.

Kylie's Song

Some said Koalas should not sing.
There's no reason why.
You can do most anything
If you really try.

Let your feelings tell you
How your song should go.
What you want and what you need,
Only you can know.

Every time you sing your song,
Sing it from your heart.
Learn it, love it, share it;
Now's the time to start.

Practice, practice, practice
'Though you're sometimes out of tune.
If you work to make it happen,
You'll be proud to sing it soon.

Everyone loved Kylie's Song.

Clarence grumbled to the kookaburra one night as they sat enjoying the evening concert, "Well, I guess Kylie is one koala who is supposed to sing."

Suddenly out of the darkness, they heard another koala voice raised in song. Turning toward the music, the startled kookaburra squawked out:

What a surprise. What a surprise.
I can't believe my ears and eyes.
Although it sounds like Kylie's song . . .

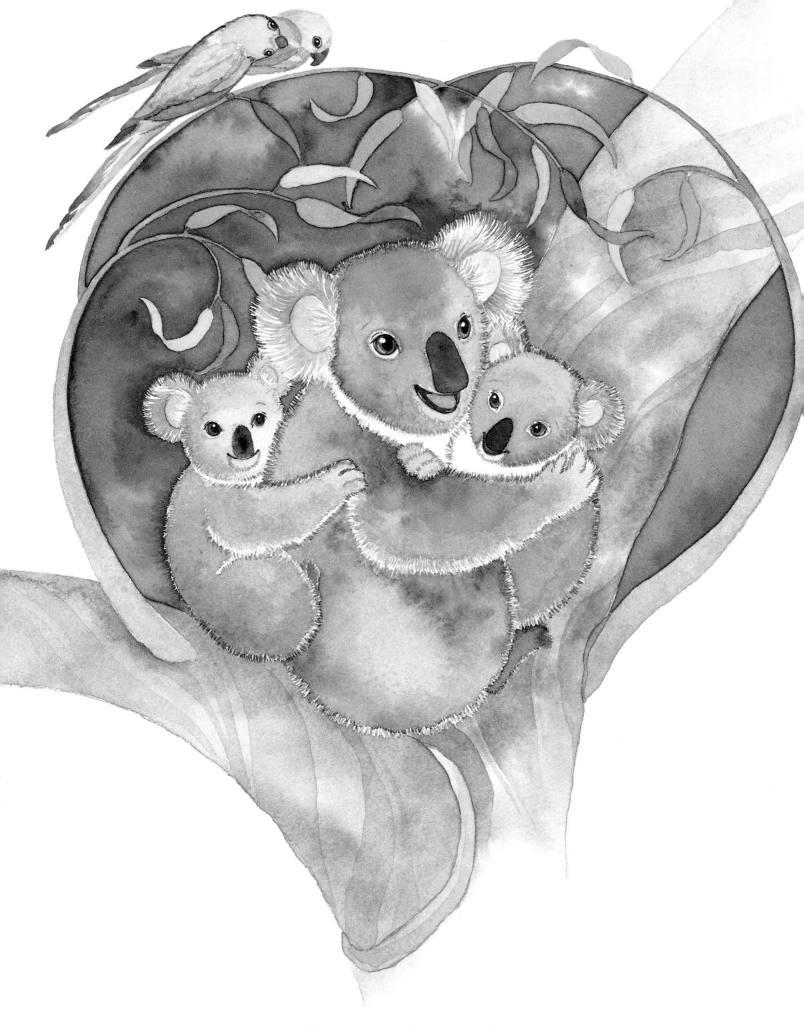

It's Mama Koala singing along!

Dear Parents and Educators:

All human beings have a unique blend of "intelligences"—verbal, musical, logical, mathematical, self- and other-awareness, spacial, artistic and kinetic. The most happy and successful people are those who go beyond the roles of accepted thinking and behavior to become fully "themselves." As they realize their own potentials more fully, they also make a greater contribution to society.

But it's easier to generalize. We all tend to make assumptions about others' capabilities based on their sex, race, ethnic group, social class or handicap. When we give in to this tendency, we not only limit their development or opportunity, we also cheat the world of their accomplishments.

Stereotyping affected the behavior of both Kylie and her mother. When Mama Koala's concern for Kylie's happiness superseded her desire to have the young koala conform, Kylie was on her way toward fulfillment. The wallaby, platypus and Willie Wagtail served as role models and instructors. Kylie did the rest. She, in turn, became a role model for Mama Koala.

To help children understand the message of *Kylie's Song,* discuss the following questions with them.

- What did Kylie love to do?

- Why did Mama Koala worry about Kylie?

- Why did Kylie stop doing the thing she loved best?

- What did Mama Koala realize as she observed Kylie after she gave up singing?

- What did Kylie learn from the wallaby and the platypus?

- What decision did Kylie make about what she would do with her life?

- What lessons did she learn from Willie Wagtail?

- What did Mama Koala learn from Kylie at the end of the story?

- What do you most love to do?

- In what ways are you like other children you know?

- In what ways are you different?

Some ways you can help children appreciate their unique talents and interests include the following:

- Be a role model for self-expression. Pursue your own interests even when they fly in the face of convention.

- Express positive attitudes about any interests a child professes. Provide as much information about and exposure to the topic as you can.

- Stop using such stereotype-inducing statements as "Take it like a man" and "That isn't ladylike." Use gender-neutral terms: police officer, not policeman; service representative, not repairman; etc.

- Ask girls to do such traditionally "male" tasks as moving furniture or fixing a flat tire. Have boys babysit or clear the table.

- Offer boys and girls equal opportunity to pursue academic, creative or athletic interests. Cheer as loudly for the girls' team as you do for the boys'.

- Acknowledge cooperation, physical strength, helpfulness and appearance equally in children of both sexes.

- Encourage girls to make decisions, be assertive and not to be afraid to make a mistake.

- Let boys know it's all right to express sadness or disappointment.

- Equate success with being the best "*you*" you can be.

- Point out stereotypical materials and attitudes in the media, the schools and other institutions. Make your disapproval known to those in charge, and encourage children to do the same.

Patty Sheehan

Patty Sheehan is a psychosynthesis counselor, speaker and writer in Albuquerque, NM, where she has lived for the past 15 years. Through teaching in early childhood programs and counselling both adults and children, she has gained a great deal of knowledge about what encourages and thwarts the development of human potential. Patty shares some of her insights in *Kylie's Song,* her first published children's book. She is currently working on several other projects, some of which, not surprisingly, are songs. Her home is near the Sandia mountains where she loves to hike and ski. Patty also enjoys travelling, participating in improvisational theater and many other creative activities.

Itoko Maeno

Itoko Maeno's earlier books for children include *Minou* by Mindy Bingham, *My Way Sally* by Mindy Bingham and Penelope Paine and *Tonia the Tree* by Sandy Stryker. Her illustrations of cosmopolitan Paris, the English countryside and the Australian outback are all accurate in detail, different in style and uniquely evocative of a particular place. Each page of *Kylie* shows her sense of design and unique use of color—children and adults will enjoy the artist's character-creations of the animals from the Australian forest. Born in Tokyo, where she received a Bachelor's degree in graphic design, she has lived in the United States since 1982. Her work has been shown at the French Embassy in Washington, D.C., and has appeared in many other books.

Books by Advocacy Press

Choices: A Teen Woman's Journal for Self-awareness and Personal Planning, by Mindy Bingham, Judy Edmondson and Sandy Stryker. Softcover, 240 pages. ISBN 0-911655-22-0. $18.95.

Challenges: A Young Man's Journal for Self-awareness and Personal Planning, by Bingham, Edmondson and Stryker. Softcover, 240 pages. ISBN 0-911655-24-7. $18.95.

More Choices, A Strategic Planning Guide for Mixing Career and Family, written by Mindy Bingham and Sandy Stryker. Softcover, 240 pages. ISBN 0-911655-28-X. $15.95.

Changes: A Woman's Journal for Self-awareness and Personal Planning, written by Mindy Bingham, Sandy Stryker and Judy Edmondson. Softcover, 240 pages. ISBN 0-911655-40-9. $18.95.

Mother-Daughter Choices: A Handbook for the Coordinator, written by Mindy Bingham, Lari Quinn and William Sheehan. Softcover, 144 pages. ISBN 0-911655-44-1. $10.95.

Women Helping Girls with Choices, written by Mindy Bingham and Sandy Stryker. Softcover, 192 pages. ISBN 0-911655-00-X. $9.95.

Minou, by Mindy Bingham, illustrated by Itoko Maeno. Hardcover with dust jacket, 64 pages with full-color illustrations throughout. ISBN 0-911655-36-0. $14.95.

My Way Sally, written by Mindy Bingham and Penelope Paine, illustrated by Itoko Maeno. Hardcover with dust jacket, 48 pages with full-color illustrations throughout. ISBN 0-911655-27-1. $14.95.

Father Gander Nursery Rhymes: The Equal Rhymes Amendment, written by Father Gander. Hardcover with dust jacket, full-color illustrations throughout, 48 pages. ISBN 0-911655-12-3. $15.95

Tonia the Tree, written by Sandy Stryker, illustrated by Itoko Maeno. Hardcover with dust jacket, 32 pages with full-color illustrations throughout. ISBN 0-911655-16-6. $13.95.

Kylie's Song, written by Patty Sheehan, illustrated by Itoko Maeno. Hardcover with dust jacket, 32 pages with full-color illustrations throughout. ISBN 0-911655-19-0. $16.95.

Berta Benz and the Motorwagen, by Mindy Bingham, illustrated by Itoko Maeno. Hardcover with dust jacket, 48 pages with full-color illustrations throughout. ISBN 0-911655-38-7. $14.95.

Time for Horatio, by Penelope Paine, illustrated by Itoko Maeno. Hardcover with dust jacket, 48 pages with full-color illustrations throughout. ISBN 0-911655-33-6. $14.95.

Mother Nature Nursery Rhymes, written by Mother Nature, illustrated by Itoko Maeno. Hardcover with dust jacket, 32 pages with full-color illustrations throughout. ISBN 0-911655-01-8. $14.95.

You can find these books at better bookstores. Or you may order them directly by sending a check for the amount shown above (California residents add appropriate sales tax), plus $4.00 each for shipping and handling, to Advocacy Press, P.O. Box 236, Dept. KS, Santa Barbara, California 93102. For your review we will be happy to send you more information on these publications. Proceeds from the sale of these books will benefit and contribute to the further development of programs for girls and young women.